A BIG DAY FOR

A Random House PICTUREBACK®

Library of Congress Cataloging-in-Publication Data
Hickle, Victoria. A big day for Brum / by Victoria Hickle ; illustrated by Mones. p. cm. — (A Random House pictureback) SUMMARY: Brum, a small antique car, has an adventure with schoolchildren on a field trip to the big Museum and then shows them the motor museum where he is usually on display.
ISBN 0-679-84494-5 [1. Automobiles—Fiction. 2. Museums—Fiction. 3. School field trips—Fiction.]
I. Mones, ill. II. Title. PZ7.H5313Br 1993 [E]—dc20 92-45105

Manufactured in the United States of America 10 9 8 7 6 5 4 3 2 1

Random House, Inc. New York, Toronto, London, Sydney, Auckland

A BIG DAY FOR
Brum™

by
Victoria Hickle

illustrated by
Mones

Random House 🏠 New York

It was Brum's day for exploring the big town. He was *brum, brum, brumming* along the pavement—when what do you think he saw?

A group of schoolchildren! They were lining up to board a bus. Brum decided to follow behind and see where they went.

Brum followed the bus as it went down this street . . .
and up that street . . . and around a corner . . .

and under a bridge . . .

and finally stopped at the Museum.

Brum knew something about museums. He lived in one. But Brum's museum was small, with old cars.

This museum looked very, very big.

"Everybody, take your buddy's hand," said the schoolteacher. "I don't want anyone getting lost."

"Wait for me!" called Brum.

But Brum couldn't drive up the wide stone staircase,
so he scooted around the building . . .

and down a ramp . . .

and through a door into the Museum.

Suddenly he heard a voice saying, "Very sorry, but no strollers allowed in the Museum." A man in a blue uniform was looking down at Brum. "I'm not a stroller," said Brum. "I'm a —"

But before he could finish, the man motioned Brum to follow him. "Right this way, if you please."

He led Brum into a small room behind the stairs and then went out, closing the door behind him.

The room was filled with carriages and strollers and bicycles.

"This is really quite silly," Brum thought. "I'm not a carriage or a stroller—and I'm certainly not a bicycle!" He scooted over to the door and beeped, hoping someone would hear and come let him out.

Luckily, just then a little boy poked his head into the room. He was carrying two lollipops, and his eyes lit up when he saw Brum.

"Daddy," said the boy.

"I think you're lost," Brum said.

"Mommy," said the boy.

"I'm sure I can help you," said Brum.

"Car!" said the boy, running after Brum as the little car rolled out of the room.

As Brum and the boy went
through the Museum, they spotted
all kinds of wonderful things:
knights in armor . . .
paintings of shipwrecks . . .

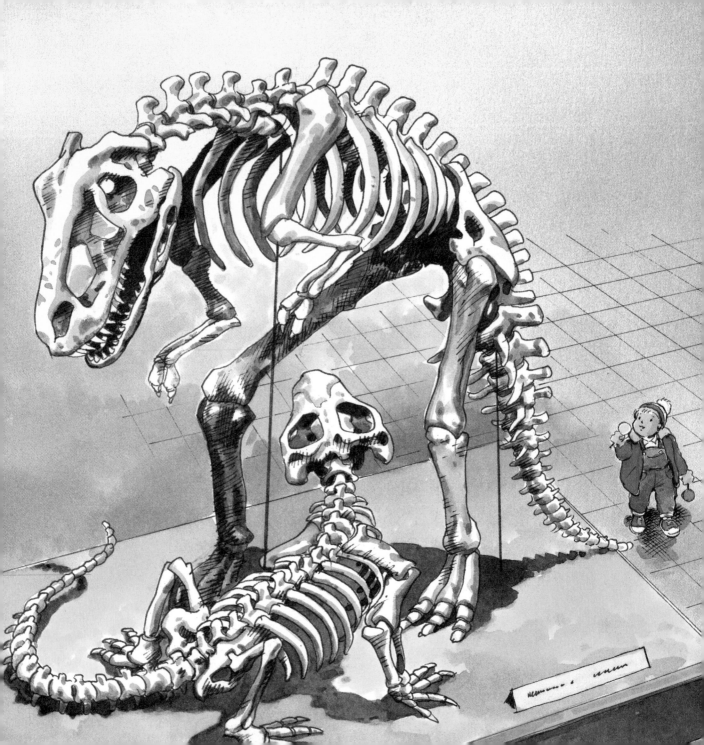

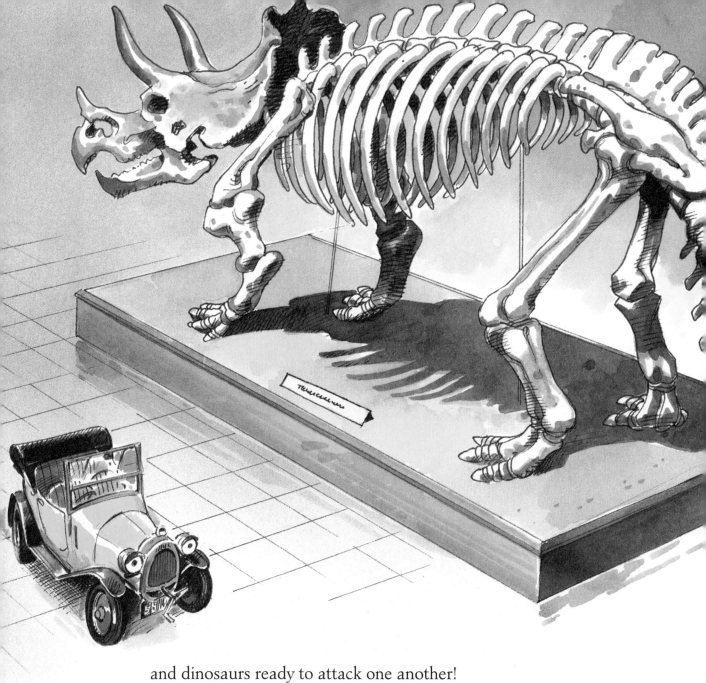

and dinosaurs ready to attack one another!

Brum would have loved to look at everything, but he knew that the first place to take the little boy to was the Information Desk.

When Brum arrived at the Information Desk, he saw the man in the blue uniform—and another man and a woman. They broke into wide smiles when they saw Brum and the little boy.

"Brian!" said the woman.

"Brum!" said the man. "We wouldn't have worried that our boy was lost if we had known Brum was with him."

"I thought I told you—no strollers allowed!" the man in the uniform said to Brum.

"Car!" said the little boy.

"That's right, he is a car—and a very special one," said Brian's father. "Thank you, Brum, for taking such good care of our boy."

"Beep-beep!" Brum happily twirled his crank around and around.

"I see I was mistaken," said the man in the uniform. "I'm sorry. However, cars aren't allowed in the Museum either. I must ask you to leave." And he ushered Brum right out of the building.

Now, what do you think happened next?

The schoolchildren were coming
down the steps of the Museum. They
were finished with their tour and were
getting ready to board the school bus . . .
but one look at Brum and they forgot
all about going back to school.

"Look, there's the little car from the motor museum!" shouted one of the children.

"Please, Brum, won't you give us a tour of *your* museum?" begged another child.

"Oh, my wheels and wipers—I'd love to!" said Brum. "Follow me, please."

"I suppose a visit to another kind of museum *would* be useful," said the children's teacher.

Brum led the way to the motor museum, and the school bus followed with the children on board.

Mike, the museum owner, was having a snooze behind the building, so Brum quietly gave the children a tour by himself.
He showed them the old cars . . .

and the old signs . . .
and the old toys and games.

"Bye-bye!" Brum said to the children when the visit was over. "Come again!"
"We will!" promised the boys and girls.

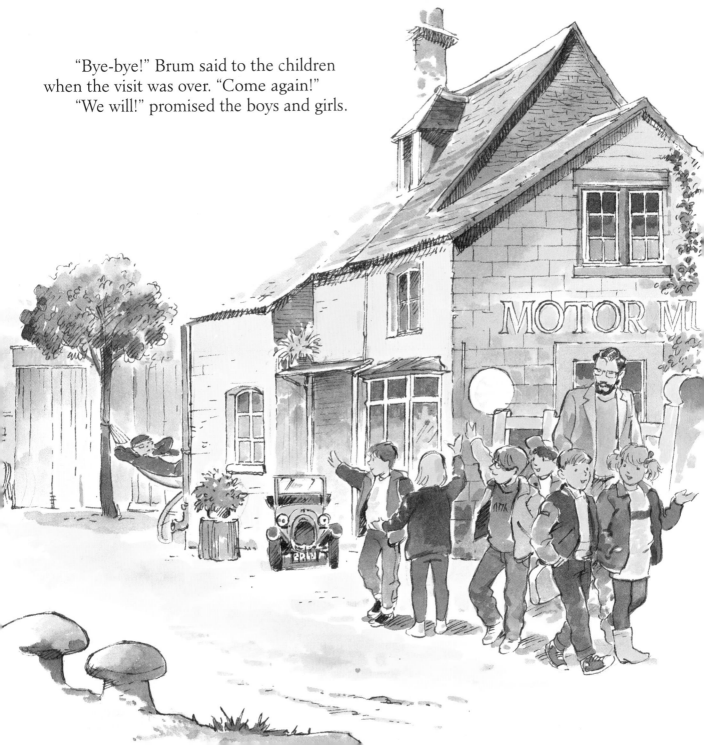

After everyone had left, Brum
brum, brum, brummed back to his spot
in the museum—and just in time,
for Mike was beginning to wake up.

"My, my, Brum," said Mike as he peered into Brum's back seat and scratched his head. "Wherever have you been today?"